M000211950

Eternal Questions:

a maybe interesting list

by

IWANNA TWAINBEE[1]

---

[1]A Faux Intellectual

Published by

Atmosphere Press

atmospherepress.com

cover design by
Senhor Tocas

HAVE
A
CONVIVIUM

twainbee.com

COPYRIGHT AND CATEGORIZATION

Library of Congress Number:
2021924582

ISBN Numbers:

Paperback:	978-1-63988-198-7
eBook:	978-1-63988-199-4
Hardcover:	978-1-63988-315-8

To Book Seller and Librarian Categorizers:

Please place under: Philosophia Commedia

To Alphabetizers:

Please place just to the right of: Twain, Mark

DEDICATION

Seldom has an author owed so much to one person.

My loving spouse is the center of my life.

I have received more help from my spouse
in every part of my life than
any spouse should ever reasonably
expect to receive from a spouse,
particularly in my case,
because my hands do so smell of mortality.[2]

---

[2] *King Lear*:

Gloucester: O, Let me kiss that hand!

Lear: Let me wipe it first. It smells of mortality.

From Joyce's *The Dead*

*Having just come on,
unsuccessfully,
to the servant girl in the pantry,
Gabriel muses that his insertion of cultural touches
into the toast he is about to give
at his Aunt Kate and Aunt Julia's
annual Christmas Party
will be an utter failure:*

Then he took from his waistcoat pocket a little paper and glanced at the headings he had made for his speech. He was undecided about the lines from Robert Browning for he feared they would be above the heads of his hearers. Some quotation that they could recognize from Shakespeare or from the Melodies[3] would be better. The indelicate clacking of the men's heels and the shuffling of their soles reminded him that their grade of culture differed from his. He would only make himself ridiculous by quoting poetry to them which they would not understand. They would think that he was airing his superior education. He would fail with them just as he had failed with the girl in the pantry. He had taken up a wrong tone. His whole speech was a mistake from first to last, an utter failure.

---

[3] Damn it, even I, the all wise and all knowing Iwanna, haven't heard of "The Melodies".

**IF YOU FIND EVEN THE
BEGINNINGS OF ANSWERS
TO THESE ETERNAL QUESTIONS,
IT WILL BE A FAR, FAR BETTER THING
THAT YOU DO
THAN YOU HAVE EVER DONE,
AND IT WILL BE
A FAR, FAR BETTER REST
THAT YOU GO TO
THAN YOU HAVE EVER KNOWN.[4]
(By the way, beware of rhetoric in this book,
particularly exaggeration).**

---

[4] Writing nine generations ago, Charles Dickens begins *A Tale of Two Cities*:

> It was the best of times, it was the worst of times, it was the age of wisdom, it was the age of foolishness, it was the epoch of belief, it was the epoch of incredulity, it was the season of Light, it was the season of Darkness, it was the spring of hope, it was the winter of despair, we had everything before us, we had nothing before us, we were all going direct to Heaven, we were all going direct the other way— in short, the period was so far like the present period, that some of its noisiest authorities insisted on its being received, for good or for evil, in the superlative degree of comparison only.

He ends the novel:

> It is a far, far better thing that I do, than I have ever done; it is a far, far better rest that I go to than I have ever known.

EXTRACTS[5]

DISCUSS WITH FRIENDS AND LOVED ONES!

TAKE QUESTIONS AT RANDOM!

GO OFF ON TANGENTS!

HAVE A CONVIVIUM!

RESIST GOOGLE!

BE PLAYFUL!

AND DON'T USE TOO MANY EXCLAMATION POINTS!

---

[5] Writing seven generations ago, Herman Melville, to get the reader loosened up, starts *Moby Dick* with a long series of "Extracts." I, Iwanna, hope the front material in this book is having the same effect on you. Three of Melville's loosening Extracts are:

> "This whale's liver was two cartloads."
> —*Stowe's Annals.*

> "Very like a whale." —*Hamlet.*

> "So be cheery, my lads, let your hearts never fail,
> While the bold harpooner is striking the whale!"
> —*Nantucket Song.*

Why do the bosses expect the underlings
to keep coming up
with creative ideas
when the bosses
so often reject
the best of those ideas?

In conversations with family members
why do we over and over trod the same ground?

How does the artist create the beautiful?

How does the artist know what is the beautiful?[6]

During the Renaissance
did any young, impoverished, Venetian gondoliers
grow up to own
shipping companies and grand palazzo?

Why do we ask our loved ones
for advice in situations
in which our minds are already made up?

---

[6] Writing four generations ago, James Joyce in *A Portrait of the Artist as a Young Man* writes:

"The object of the artist is the creation of the beautiful. What the beautiful is is another question."

Are our delusions about our egos
the source of our suffering?

Will suffering provide enlightenment?

Will enlightenment
reduce suffering?

Does the amount of suffering change?

Will more or less suffering
make the world better?

If life is to be mostly
ignorance and suffering,
how do we know
when we may for a moment set aside
our ignorance and suffering and
guiltlessly enjoy the sweet parts?

If another 9/11 occurs
will there be an outburst of patriotism?

Should a drunk driver with zero intent to kill
but who does kill
receive a harsher penalty
than a drunk driver
with the same zero level of intent but
who hurts no one?[7]

How bad must the symptoms be
before we keep the kids home from school?

---

[7] Writing ninety-eight generations ago, Aristotle in the *Nicomachean Ethics* recommends double penalties for crimes with bad outcomes.

Is happiness a feeling of conscious vitality?

Is conscious vitality,
even if directed only at our vocation,
sufficient for a happy life?

What is "sufficient" conscious vitality anyway?

Over the long pull
will productivity gains ever
stay ahead of inflation?

When we see our neighbor
riding her bike with her dog,
and the dog is running and panting on a leash,
is it better to be silent
at the expense
of the dog, or
is it better
to call out the cruelty of the neighbor
toward the dog
at the expense of
the relationship with the neighbor?

Why is it so hard to focus on the art and not the artist?

Is there anything more frustrating
than having a good idea and then forgetting it?

What is gracious living?

Are charts, symbols, equations, tables and graphs
necessary to an understanding of Economics?

Is the hangover worth it?

Even if only just for practice,
should we at least occasionally forage?

Does capitalism cause alienation?

If capitalism leads to such good things as
inequality, higher standard of living for all,
individuality, innovation, and human trust,
but it also leads to such bad things as
inequality, alienation, exploitation of labor, and
misallocation of value due to failure to recognize
that the value of a thing is equal to
the value of the labor put into it,
is capitalism still worth it?[8]

Just how much alienation is really out there?

What will be the costs of a revolt against capitalism?

---

[8] Writing eight generations ago, Thomas Carlyle sees it all
coming in his essay, "Signs of the Times":

> What wonderful accessions have thus been made,
> and are still making, to the physical power of
> mankind; how much better fed, clothed, lodged and,
> in all outward respects, accommodated men now
> are, or might be, by a given quantity of labour, is a
> grateful reflection which forces itself on every one.
> What changes, too, this addition of power is
> introducing into the Social System; how wealth has
> more and more increased, and at the same time
> gathered itself more and more into masses,
> strangely altering the old relations, and increasing
> the distance between the rich and the poor, will be a
> question for Political Economists, and a much more
> complex and important one than any they have yet
> engaged with.

What is the good life?

What is the virtuous life?

Are they different?

Does any difference matter?

Does having a life's purpose
usually make a good life?

Does encountering danger, surprise, and unpleasantness
usually make a good life?

Does less stress and more safety
usually make a good life?

Does more culture
usually make a good life?

Is there a human soul?

If so, is there a recycle center?

If there is both a human soul and an after-life,
once we are dead
do we only move on, or
do we get a bleacher seat from which we may
observe our still living friends and loved ones
engage in their on-going shenanigans?

If God (or Karma) takes care of fools and drunks, and
if a lass gets sober,
will God (or Karma) still take care of her?

How do we know
whether the critic is leading us to do our own thinking or
is doing our thinking for us?

Why memorize?

Why do male leaders of nations
so often attack their neighbors?

Why do female leaders of nations
so seldomly attack their neighbors?

Is the French approach,
vive la différence,
the best approach?

Why do men tease and joke around so?

Why do women squabble so?[9]

---

[9] Writing four generations ago, James Joyce in *Ulysses*, in the chapter known as "Lestrygonians", describes the thoughts of his elder protagonist, Leopold Bloom, as Bloom wanders around Dublin, Ireland. Bloom sees a woman pass another woman. He responds in an internal monologue:

> See the eye that woman gave her, passing. Cruel. The unfair sex.

Hamlet says in reference to his mother, the Queen, after he is pretty sure she knows her current husband has killed her prior husband, Hamlet's very father, and her current husband is thus a usurping King and she has married him anyway because she likes being Queen: "Frailty, thy name is woman."

Writing four generations ago, Ford Madox Ford in *The Good Soldier* calls out the "curious, discounting eye which one woman can turn on another."

Writing nine generations ago, Emily Brontë in *Wuthering Heights* gives us a nice squabbling women paragraph. The

Is humanity perfectible?

If humanity is perfectible
will perfection come
from a better designed society?

If so, who will be the designer?

Is there any truth at all to the Nirvana Fallacy, that is,
the idea that if we change societal systems
human nature will be different?

How do we stop ourselves
from judging others by stereotype?

Is the business cycle inevitable or
is it caused by government policy?

Is the everywhere fog of the court system
so apt a metaphor for all of government policy
that government should attempt no policy at all?

---

servant-narrator, Nelly, is talking about the antics
between another servant, Zillah, and Catherine, the young
mistress:

> She thinks Catherine haughty, and does not like her,
> I can guess by her talk. My young lady asked some
> aid of her when she first came; but Mr. Heathcliff
> told her to follow her own business, and let his
> daughter-in-law look after herself; and Zillah
> willingly acquiesced, being a narrow-minded, self-
> ish woman. Catherine evinced a child's annoyance
> at this neglect; repaid it with contempt, and thus
> enlisted my informant among her enemies, as
> securely as if she had done her some great wrong.

Are we here as a result of
Random Accidents or the Hand of God?

Between Random Accidents and the Hand of God
is there a path in the middle?

Do all people on both sides of the God question
have in their back pocket
just a touch of doubt?

Will having failed to have thought about God
during life
affect our chances for something, anything,
after death?

Should we live into Pascal's wager,
that is,
should we believe in God
because with the stakes so high
it is the safer choice?

If we live into Pascal's wager,
but only as a chess move toward God,
and not out of sincerity,
will God keep Her side of the bargain?

Does Pascal have it all wrong because
God does exist and
She loves us so much
that She will at death take us into Her arms
even if we have rejected Her in life?

How do we know the way?

If we are in a yellow wood
will taking the diverging road
make all the difference?

How often do the truly dishonorable
truly repent and then
permanently reform?

Is there a limit to economic growth?[10]

Are pawn shops moral?

If a proposition cannot be proved false,
is it true?

Does Apple have a duty to reduce the price of iPhones?

Does Apple have a duty to increase the price of iPhones?

Quis custodiet ipsos custodes?[11]

high house low boat high car?

low house high boat low car?

low apartment high boat high pick-up?

low apartment no boat high car?

For whom do we garden?

Is humility the greatest virtue?

If not, what is?

---

[10] Every year on the Wednesday before Thanksgiving the Wall Street Journal runs an editorial from the 1960's written by a wise old editor named Vermont Royster. Therein appears the following sentence: "America, though many know it not, is one of the great underdeveloped countries of the world; what it reaches for exceeds by far what it has grasped."

[11] Who watches the watchman?

What in us stops us
from telling our boss,
to her face,
even if it is true,
that she is a RAGING...?

Why do we so often treat our boss
better than our own family members, that is,
why do we *never* tell our boss she is a raging...,
even though we will *often* tell our own husband
that he is a goddamn bastard?[12]

How does the museum curator properly decide
when to pitch the old and exhibit the new?

When we visit the Art Museum
is it worthwhile
to read the blurbs
next to the paintings?

Will learning
to speak and write
with proper grammar,
particularly after we have finished formal schooling,
make both us smile and our interlocutors smile?

How may we live in humble gratitude?

---

[12] One could write and study and think for years and not say it as simply as Emily Brontë:

> I believed a person who could plan the turning of her fits of passion to account, beforehand, might, by exerting her will, manage to control herself tolerably.

What energizes a mob?

What enervates a mob?

If a lad or lass kisses a woman,
and then whispers in her ear,
"You have witchcraft in your lips, Kate,"
does that make the wooing a sure thing?[13]

How may we stay in relationship
with our children—even when our children
are acting like idiots?[14]

How far should those in authority go
to make things fair?

Is making things fair
the right goal for those in authority?

What is it about stogies?

---

[13] In *Henry V*, a Shakespeare history play about events which occurred in the early 1400's, the English give the French a good licking at the battle of Agincourt, and the English King goes to the French Palace to woo Katherine, the French princess. He asks her if she will "have him" and she says "Dat is as it shall please de *roi mon père*," (her father, The King). He responds: "Nay, it will please him well, Kate; it shall please him, Kate." A few lines later "patiently and yielding", he kisses her. He pauses, savoring the moment and says: "You have witchcraft in your lips, Kate." She yields.

[14] Let's have at it from the other perspective too: How does a girl stay in relationship with her parents when her parents are acting like idiots?

Does natural law exist?

If natural law exists
does it come
from God, from Woman, or
from some other mysterious source?

What the hell is natural law anyway?

Should we be more delighted
on the winter solstice
when Christmas is close and
the long days are all in the fore-view, or
should we be more delighted
on the summer solstice
when the longest day is present in all its glory and
the short days are all in the fore-view?

Are freedom of speech and freedom of religion
the most critical rights
to the maintenance of liberty?

What of property?

What of association?

What of the rest of the rights in the
Bill of Rights?

Is our right to ourselves,
whatever that is,
a right?

How much and what should we give beggars?

Are the social sciences science?

Better to have street smarts or book smarts?

At formal occasions
should we make the children dress appropriately
or should we just be glad they showed up at all?

Is life so meaningless and absurd
that we should commit suicide?

Does our not committing suicide
guide us to the answers
to all other philosophical questions? [15] [16]

How may we more often
say yes than say no?

As we reach
the top rung of the ladder of our success,
how often do we find
we are on the wrong ladder, and/or
that our ladder is leaning on the wrong wall?

Is the greatest of creatures the dog?

Does Christmas come too often?

---

[15] Writing three generations ago, French philosopher and novelist Albert Camus set the avant-garde, absurdist, existentialist, European smart set agog by asking these last two questions about suicide. He and his buddies apparently saw the questions as new and original. Perhaps they were not familiar with...

To be or not be? That is the question.

[16] I, Iwanna, am pretty sure, darn it, that after we have committed suicide there will be no convivia with our still living friends to discuss these Eternal Questions.

When, if ever, does appropriate attention
to obtaining social éclat
descend into shameless social climbing?

When, if ever, does appropriate attention
to looking our best every day
descend into shameless vanity?[17]

When, if ever, does attention
to making money
descend into shameless greed?

Why do
siblings, parents and children, and sometimes spouses,
so often get entangled in
reflexive contrarian syndrome? [18]

Better to keep the kids in one school all K-12, or
better to move them about a bit for fresh starts?

---

[17] In *Hamlet* the old but not wholly foolish counselor, Polonius, puts it this way, not missing a dig at the Frogs:

Costly thy habit as thy purse can buy,
But not express'd in fancy; rich, not gaudy;
For the apparel oft proclaims the man,
And they in France of the best rank and station
Are of a most select and generous chief in that.

[18] I, Iwanna, have articulated and will soon acquire a Ph.D. for my dissertation on "Reflexive Contrarian Syndrome," which is when members of the same family, mostly siblings, but sometimes parents and children and/or sometimes spouses, reflexively disagree with one another, regardless of the merits of the issue at hand.

How many 2nd chances for our spouses?

How many 2nd chances for our lovers?

How bad must be the behavior to use up a chance?

Why do some of us reflexively
support or oppose the positions
of established institutions and organizations,
without regard to the merits
of the particular position at issue?

In hiring
how do we distinguish
between the slick interviewer and
the good performer?

In buying
how do we distinguish
between the slick saleswoman and
the good product?

How do we recognize a good product
even when the saleswoman is a boob?

How comes the giraffe's neck to be so long?

After we have accumulated our great financial fortune,
what shall we do with it?

If there are no
spirits or angels
why does it so often seem that there are
spirits and angels?

Why such disdain for
Amway and Mary Kay?

Why on vacation is time so tight?

In foreign relations
what factors enable us to tell
the good gals from the bad gals?

When our President is considering
pulling our country out of a foreign entanglement, and
when we have been honest in helping
the good gals fight the bad gals
in that other country,
how does she decide whether to go or stay?

May our leader morally pull out of another country,
leaving behind those who were helpful to us,
knowing our helpers will likely be
slaughtered as collaborators?

Why get into these situations in the first place?

Should our President maintain friendly relations
with the leaders of other countries who
enslave, torture, imprison, silence and kill
both their own people and other people's peoples?

Come next year
what will be the
interest rate?

Does enhanced individualism
lead to more barbarism or to more civilization?

When Princess Diana
wore cropped pants
why did every other
woman in the world
go out and buy
cropped pants?

Because organ transplants
are not available to everyone everywhere
should we not do them at all?

If a healthy 25-year-old walks in the hospital
and five 75-year-olds are lying in misery upstairs
such that they will only continue living
if we kill the 25-year-old and
harvest and distribute her organs to them,
should we do it?

How do we articulate what would be wrong with that?

How do we balance
egoism's urge to withdraw from society
with, if effected,
the resulting loss to society?

Should a leader seek the truth
in her organization
by speaking directly
to those down the ranks, or
does such direct contact
improperly undermine the effectiveness
of the middle level management team?

Does travel lead to wisdom?

Other than leading others to think we are cool
what is the purpose of reporting our travels
on social media?

What are some of the ways
history and human nature teach us
that one woman should not have
unchecked power over other women?

Are the purposes of jewelry and tattoos about the same?

Why so many tattoos on boobs and moobs?

Will women ever quit gazing
at moobs?

Does women's obsession
with gazing at moobs
come from
nature or nurture?

Will men ever be relieved
of their ambivalence
about women gazing at their moobs?

Will gorgeous men
ever lose their advantage
in seeking out and marrying
rich women?

Will plain men ever quit
hating gorgeous men?

Is it true for men that:
in their aughts and teens they need good parents,
in their twenties and thirties they need good looks,
in their forties and fifties they need good cheer, and
after that all they need is cash?

What are the female equivalents?

Do older men remain attractive
only for their money, power and influence?

Who killed the Kennedys
or after all was it you and me?

How do we distinguish,
in ourselves and in others
genuine piety from faux piety?

How do we bring nature's peace
into the bustle of everyday life? [19]

When we adults are vainly attempting to impart
to our youngsters whatever wisdom
we have gained so far,
why do they so seldom listen?

What are the better ways to get them to listen?

Is it the individual, is it history, or is it society
which is responsible for our problems,
or, if it is all three, what are the proportions of fault?

If all the electronics on the plane twizzle fizzle out,
will the pilot still be able to land the plane?

With vaccines how do we handle the free rider problem?

---

[19] Writing eight generations ago, William Wordsworth in the first four lines of his sonnet "The World is Too Much with Us" captures the tension between one's economic life and the loss of the love of nature which too much attention to economic life may cause:

> The world is too much with us; late and soon,
> Getting and spending, we lay waste our powers;
> Little we see in Nature that is ours;
> We have given our hearts away, a sordid boon.

(Footnoting my footnotes I note that Russ Roberts of Econ-Talk has brought me many poems and many questions).

How do we balance obedience and free will?[20]

To whom do we owe obedience anyway?

---

[20] Genesis has the Judeo-Christian tradition's first exercise of free will leading to a first great moment of excuse making and covering up. Adam and Eve have eaten the apple. They tie fig leaves over their parts recently recognized as private. They hear God tromping about and they hide in the trees. God calls them and they emerge, sheepishly. The following ensues, King James Version:

> "Who told thee that thou wast naked? Hast thou eaten of the tree, whereof I commanded thee that thou shouldest not eat?"

> And the man said, "The woman whom thou gavest to be with me, she gave me of the tree, and I did eat."

> And the Lord God said unto the woman, "What is this that thou hast done?"

> And the woman said, "The serpent beguiled me, and I did eat."

Writing 15 generations ago, John Milton in *Paradise Lost* swaps out the order of "beguiled" and "me" and thereby not only makes the sentence scan in iambic pentameter, but also, in my view, makes it read with more grace:

> The serpent me beguiled and I did eat.

Thus a switch of two words by one of English Literature's TOP FIVE authors (Chaucer, Shakespeare, Dickens and Twain being the other four, say I, Iwanna), has made all the difference.

What percentage of rock stars are in it
mainly for money, fame, and girls?

What percentage of religious leaders are in it
mainly for money, fame, and girls?

Were the Rolling Stones in it
mainly for money, fame, and girls?[21]

For older professors
is it too late for money, fame, and girls
and is all they have left the vacations?

Will there ever be less traffic
on the Washington Beltway?

Is it moral that people
with bad credit in their past
pay more
for credit in their future?

Who thrives after the revolution?

Was it better under the Czars?

How often does a restaurant make it
on atmosphere alone?

Does an artificially intelligent vacuum cleaner
aspire to be
an artificially intelligent driverless car?

What are the pluses and minuses
of living by the precautionary principle?

---

[21] Jagger admits it to be so in a quote on the wall at the
Cleveland Rock and Roll Hall of Fame.

Why do scientists sometimes descend into politics
with a resulting cheapening of the brand?

Will science answer all the questions?

Does science answer questions of morality and values?

If science
answers all the questions
will religion cease?

Is the existence of beer
proof of the existence of God?
Wine? Bourbon? Pot? Heroin? Women?

May the world be made over?[22]

Are some of us
better than others of us?

Are some of us
morally superior to others of us?

Are "better" and "morally superior"
different?

If some of us are better than others of us,
what are the appropriate criteria
to make the judgment?

Skills? Aspirations? Thoughts? Behaviors? Intentions?

Will the Orient and the Occident
ever achieve mutual understanding?

---

[22] Writing twelve generations ago, immigrant and patriot
Thomas Paine says the American Revolution was doing
exactly that.

Why do we so often betray
those whom we love the most?[23]

How do we know whether and if so when
to forgive a friend or loved one
who has betrayed us?

On relations between the genders,
what are the effects of birth control so far,
that is, what are the effects of
copulation without population?

As times and circumstances change
does the tithe stay about right?

Should our tithe be before or after tax?

---

[23] Writing twenty-eight generations ago in the first, *Inferno* section of his *Divine Comedy*, Dante Alighieri places in the final, bottom ring of hell three people, Judas Iscariot, Brutus and Cassius. Judas seems to have a lock on the Christian's tradition's position as number one betrayer, and the other two conspired against Caesar. For years I struggled to understand why, despite his betrayal of Caesar, Dante would put Brutus, the noblest Roman of them all, in the bottom circle. I have always thought of Brutus as a good guy because he killed Caesar to save Rome from tyranny, or at least that was his unfilled aspiration. Perhaps Dante is telling us not to betray our friends. On the other hand, some Dante scholars suggest that Dante may have put Brutus there because he destroyed God's plan to have Caesar rule Rome. I, Iwanna, find that theory too convoluted.

Why is it true,
except in politics,
that doing a favor creates
a greater feeling of friendship
than receiving a favor?[24]

Are the Declaration of Independence and
the United States Constitution
worth defending against all enemies
foreign and domestic?

If not, have they ever been worth so defending?

If so, will they always be worth so defending?

Is it OK to be a collaborator
if you are collaborating
with the Americans?

Are animals doing their own experiments on us?

---

[24] Speaking one hundred and one generations ago, Pericles, leader of Athens, says in his funeral oration for the year's dead warriors, (Jowett translation, 1881):

> Now he who confers a favor is the firmer friend, because he would rather by kindness keep alive the in his feelings, because he knows that in requiting another's generosity he will not be winning gratitude but only paying a debt.

Writing four generations ago, Dale Carnegie in *How to Win Friends & Influence People*, an early player in the business advice genre, says that to make a friend one should accept a favor, not do a favor.

Why do law schools
hire as professors
persons who don't practice law and
who are therefore unaware
of the legal profession's
vast unwritten code
of customs and procedures?

Did pre-literate civilizations
have property rights, and if so,
what do we speculate were the sources and contours
of those property rights?

If your nation is descending into tyranny
and you see the dictator's jack-booted thugs
coming right now for your neighbor,
(likely in the middle of the night),
should you emerge from the safety of your home and
shoot the jack-booted thugs at your own personal risk,
or should you hide inside your own home
in the hope of saving
your own family for another day?

When giving a speech
is it better to read from a prepared text or to proceed
ex tempore?

Do pretty women walk faster?

If buying friends
didn't work in middle school
why do leaders think it will work
in foreign affairs?

Are some people so smart
that they are coming around to dumb again?

Does wisdom begin
when we accept that we are not special?

Does happiness begin
when we cease caring what others think of us?

Does wisdom begin
when we cease caring what others think of us? [25]

Is it the players or the coach?

Is prejudice ever right?[26]

---

[25] Writing just now, Amor Towles in *A Gentleman in Moscow* lays out self-aggrandizing pomp:

> For however decisive the Bolsheviks' victory had been over the privileged classes on behalf of the Proletariat, they would be having banquets soon enough. Perhaps there would not be as many as there had been under the Romanovs—no autumn dances or diamond jubilees—but they were bound to celebrate something, whether the centennial of *Das Kapital* or the silver anniversary of Lenin's beard. Guest lists would be drawn up and shortened. Invitations would be engraved and delivered. Then, having gathered around a grand circle of tables, the new statesmen would nod their heads in order to indicate to a waiter (without interrupting the long-winded fellow on his feet) that, yes, they would have a few more spears of asparagus.

> For pomp is a tenacious force. And a wily one too.

[26] Writing three generation ago, Richard Weaver, a southern but still wise philosopher, says yes.

What attributes of a society will result in
the common people respecting and
living in peace with the cultivated classes,
or is that scenario too absurd
to be worth considering?

What attributes of a military organization will result in
the enlisted personnel respecting and following
the officers with faithfulness and eagerness, or
is the military already getting that outcome
better than the rest of us, and thus we
should just learn from and emulate
the military's approach?

Is ceasing to fear death
the beginning of freedom?

What should we fear?

What is the benefit of fearing what we fear?

Other than solving the prisoner's dilemma,
what are the purposes of the omertà,
the mafia law of silence?

Should the poor pay taxes?

Why do those who are religious
receive contempt and ridicule
from the non-religious, but
the non-religious receive
only contempt
from the religious?

To what should a 21-year-old aspire?

To what should a 31-year-old aspire?

During negotiations
why do some think it smart to tell
the other side what is in the other side's
best interest?

Why don't the conservative think tanks get together and
have their smartest gals write a draft tax code which will
raise a reasonable amount of revenue,
be reasonably fair,
be able to be administered with relative ease,
be comprehensible, and
nudge no one in any particular direction?

Does male anxiety result
from the impending, inevitable
loss of sexual desirability?

Does female anxiety diminish
upon the birth of the child?

When does one people's conquest of another people
become a *fait accompli* and
so become no longer worth fighting about?

Does the conduct of the new rulers
affect the calculation?

Does the conduct of the new and old populations
affect the calculation?

Does the level of productivity
under the new rulers
affect the calculation?

How do we know when to treat a dumb idea
with respect and
when to get frustrated and tell the proponent off?

Power or intimacy: Which is the greatest aphrodisiac?

Does the rate of adultery change?

On weekends is it better to go away
to our country retreat and
enjoy nature's tranquility, or
is it better to stay home
and party with our hometown friends?

How much human conduct
remains driven
by animal instincts?

Are there acrophobic squirrels?

Are there agoraphobic bison?

Are there ophidiophobic mongeese? (mongooses?)

When a woman makes an errant comment,
and then tries to excuse it as a joke,
how do we know if she is really joking?

It was a dark and stormy night,
with no one around,
and so why was it
more serious
to run straight through the red light
but less serious
to make a verboten right on red?

Is today more important than tomorrow, or
is tomorrow more important than today?

May airline executives be moral *and*
allow in-flight peanuts?

Why do upper class kids dress like lower class kids?

Is any human pecking order fair?

Is there always a human pecking order?

How do we gain sufficient self-control
to extend our time horizon and so
defer immediate gratification and so
provide a higher standard of living
for our grandchildren?

How hard should we push the little twerps?

Or should we just blow off the little twerps
and take a vacation to Tahiti so we can
post pictures of our lovely selves on FB?

Is there objective truth,
or is it all just
moral relativism and shifting sands?

How often does a sophist's rhetoric
lead to objective truth?[27]

---

[27] A libertarian, someone who believes in individual freedom to a fault, walks into a bar owned by a sophist, someone overly twisted up by thinking about Eternal Questions. There is a fireplace. The libertarian and the sophist argue. The sophist says there can be no objective truth. The dispute becomes heated. The sophist finally loses his temper, picks up a hot poker and only at the last moment stops himself from poking the libertarian. The libertarian wins the argument by stating that it is an objective truth that a host should not almost poke his guest with a hot poker. Edmonds and Eidinow tell this tale in *Wittgenstein's Poker*.

Are country rubes rubes?

Are urban relativists
more wise than country rubes?

What percentage of the time
is life unfair?

How do we accept our lot
even as we try to improve our lot?

When we are around family
how do we steel ourselves
to neither roll our eyes nor
murmur under our breath?

How has the separation of church and state affected
Western Civilization, and, (where applied),
Worldwide Civilization?

Is the triumph of the individual over the state
the greatest contribution of Western Civilization?

On the 1 to 10 scale
with 1 shameful and 10 glorious,
where stands Western Civilization?

Should a baseball umpire who has just
inadvertently called a ball a strike
call the next strike a ball, or
would that overcompensate?

How does that question apply to the great principles
of Western Civilization?

Is there a line between
what we are to render unto Caesar and
what we are to render unto God, (if God exists)?

Is it fair that good saleswomen
make more money?

Is it fair that wallflowers
get less dances?

Is it fair that children
of more motivated parents
have greater success
at life's endeavors?

Must we hold our temper
every single time, and
if not, when, and why not?

What percentage of the population
is too dumb and/or incompetent
to achieve
the dignity of self-reliance?

Will forcing our children
to make their beds and pick up their socks
make them more likely
to make their beds and pick up their socks
when they are adults?

Why do parents often
give more money
to their spendthrift, wayward children than they give
to their non-spendthrift, prudent children?

Should the non-spendthrift, prudent children
graciously accept the situation
because they should be thankful
they are who they are and that they are not
the spendthrift, wayward children?

When there are so many laws
that the law has become incomprehensible
is it still the Rule of Law?

How may we increase the flowering
of our imagination?[28]

What is the source of morality?

What is the best approach
to imparting a moral center
to our children?

How and why is sex equated with death?

How do we find our own line
between frugal and cheap?

---

[28] Writing three generations ago, John Steinbeck in *Sweet Thursday* describes the use of imagination:

The flame of conception seems to flare and go out, leaving man shaken, and at once happy and afraid. There's plenty of precedent of course. Everyone knows about Newton's apple. Charles Darwin and his *Origin of Species* flashed complete in one second, and he spent the rest of his life backing it up; and the theory of relativity occurred to Einstein in the time it takes to clap your hands. This is the great mystery of the human mind—the inductive leap. Everything falls into place, irrelevancies relate, dissonance becomes harmony, and nonsense wears a crown of meaning. But the clarifying leap springs from the rich soil of confusion, and the leaper is not unfamiliar with pain.

May we find enlightenment
in confusion and paradox?

May we find happiness
in confusion and paradox?

Does formal learning lead to enlightenment?

Does formal learning lead to
recognition and acceptance of paradox?

What are the basic values
from which we derive human dignity?

Is an individual's human nature mutable or immutable?

Is all humanity's human nature mutable or immutable?

Is socialism the winner designée?

If we cease studying the past
do we become nomads in the present?

If the 9/11 Pennsylvania plane had not crashed but had
instead headed right at the White House
should the Marine fighter pilot chasing it
have waited until the last moment
but should she then have followed
the Vice-President's order to shoot it down?

How often does one bad seed bring down a great family?

Are art gallery openings
more for people or
more for art?

Does modernity's noise
cause a loss of reflection?

(Don't answer so quickly).

How can the United States military
remain on point day after day
when the interval between,
say, Pearl Harbor and 9/11,
was 60 years?

What attributes make a patrician?

Is our desire to throw off our clothes
to enjoy the happiness of nudity
based on our subconscious desire
to throw off original sin?

How may we distinguish
a faux intellectual
from a real intellectual?

Is there anything more enthralling
than the exercise of influence?[29]

How about the exercise
of responsibility responsibly?

If all of us are
thieves, liars and hypocrites,
how do we discern the line where
we must cut off contact
with a thieving, lying, hypocritical
lover, friend, family member or acquaintance?

For our kids may we take every advantage possible?

---

[29] Writing five generations ago, Oscar Wilde in *The Picture of Dorian Gray*, with perhaps more refinement, phrases it in the indicative mood, "There was something terribly enthralling in the exercise of influence."

Why do some otherwise sane people
lose the line
between the real world and
the virtual world?

While on the way to the airport
how do we know whether
we have turned off the burner?

In what order do we rank our duties to
our parents, our siblings,
our bosses, our subordinates,
our friends, our enemies,
our mentors, our mentees,
our teachers, our students,
our children and our spouses?

Will the vision of a world
which has broken the cycle
of peace, military buildup,
surprise attack, war profiteering, and then
slaughter on one side and slaughter on the other side
until one side is too slaughtered
to get up and fight another day,
ever come about?

May we thus ever truly
guide our feet into the way of peace?[30]

Do churchgoers behave
incrementally better?

Why don't other countries adopt the U.S. Constitution?

---

[30] Apostle Luke, not Cool Hand Luke. Or are they the same?

How do we, as hostesses,
know how to make the party zip?

How do we, as hostesses, know when
to end it by cutting off the music and the booze?

How do we best select
she who will have the final say
at home?
at work?
in government?
in battle?
in seances?

Why does it seem,
relative to other times and places in history,
that just now America's
middle-class and lower-class youth,
don't seem to be aspiring to
form families,
own homes,
save for retirement,
develop careers, and
make their children the heirs,
of America's traditions
of individualism and self-reliance?

If real intellectuals are so smart,
why are the articles they write
in their scholarly journals
so incomprehensible?

At retirement better to decamp for warmer climes, or
better to stay put with the old friends?

During a surprise attack
is it better to shut the doors of the fort
leaving an unhappy few of our compatriots outside [31] and

---

[31] King Henry V in his St. Crispian Speech in *Henry V* before the battle of Agincourt knows that his side has the long bow and the French do not, so he is a touch cocky:

Westmorland:

> O that we now had here
> But one ten thousand of those men in England
> That do no work to-day!

King:

> What's he that wishes so?
> My cousin, Westmorland? No, my fair cousin;
> If we are mark'd to die, we are enough
> To do our country loss; and if to live,
> The fewer men, the greater share of honour.
> God's will! I pray thee, wish not one man more.
> By Jove, I am not covetous for gold,
> Nor care I who doth feed upon my cost;
> It yearns me not if men my garments wear;
> Such outward things dwell not in my desires.
> But if it be a sin to covet honour,
> I am the most offending soul alive.
> No, faith, my coz, wish not a man from England.
> God's peace! I would not lose so great an honour
> As one man more methinks would share from me
> For the best hope I have. O, do not wish one more!
> Rather proclaim it, Westmorland, through my host,
> That he which hath no stomach to this fight,
> Let him depart; his passport shall be made,

And crowns for convoy put into his purse;
We would not die in that man's company
That fears his fellowship to die with us.
This day is call'd the feast of Crispian.
He that outlives this day, and comes safe home,
Will stand a tip-toe when this day is nam'd,
And rouse him at the name of Crispian.
He that shall live this day, and see old age,
Will yearly on the vigil feast his neighbours,
And say "To-morrow is Saint Crispian."
Then will he strip his sleeve and show his scars,
And say "These wounds I had on Crispin's day."
Old men forget; yet all shall be forgot,
But he'll remember, with advantages,
What feats he did that day. Then shall our names,
Familiar in his mouth as household words—
Harry the King, Bedford and Exeter,
Warwick and Talbot, Salisbury and Gloucester—
Be in their flowing cups freshly rememb'red.
This story shall the good man teach his son;
And Crispin Crispian shall ne'er go by,
From this day to the ending of the world,
But we in it shall be rememberèd—
We few, we happy few, we band of brothers;
For he to-day that sheds his blood with me
Shall be my brother; be he ne'er so vile,
This day shall gentle his condition;
And gentlemen in England now a-bed
Shall think themselves accurs'd they were not here,
And hold their manhoods cheap whiles any speaks
That fought with us upon Saint Crispin's day.

so exposed to disastrous slaughter, or
is it better to keep the doors open
and so let in the late-comers, but then by definition
leave ourselves and our compatriots already inside
exposed to disastrous slaughter?[32]

When a Lady sets out to write
Eternal Questions: a maybe interesting list
how does she not be led
into temptation
and end up creating
Rhetorical Questions: a surely boring list?

How am I, Iwanna, doing on that?

Question Authority?

Every time?

How do we know?

Why do members of today's upper class
deny that they are in the upper class and
claim they are just in the middle class?

---

[32] Writing eighty generations ago, Virgil in the *Aeneid*, Book XI, Ferry Translation, a poem about the founding of Rome, places the Latins in their fort facing a siege. They face this very dilemma:

> Latins were dying, gasping away their lives,
> And other Latins, in panic, got the gates closed,
> To keep more Trojans out, and they didn't dare
> In spite of their desperate pleadings, to open them
> Again for comrades who were left outside,
> And miserable mutual slaughter took place.

While we have yet to shuffle off our mortal coil
how much of our inheritance
from our rich, dead parents
should we give
to our adult children?

Is the United States Marine Corps'
firm principle:
nemo reside,
the duty to leave no woman behind,
even if we must sacrifice the many to retrieve the one,
a wise principle?

Why is there so much more monetary value
put on an original painting by an old master
than on a good fake of the same painting,
when a good fake
(or, to use a more polite term,
a good "reproduction"),
is indistinguishable
to all but the most trained eye, and
for everyone else
the value of the painting
should come from the enrichment
we get from looking at the image and
not from the status
of owning an original?

Is it moral to torture one woman to get her to talk
in order to save the lives of many?

How about to kill her to save the lives of many?

Even in religion, (or mostly in religion?)
does it always come down to the money?

If a nuclear submarine captain,
under strict orders never to surface,
has learned that a surface ship
is about to sink with the loss of all hands,
and that she can save all of them
by disobeying her orders and surfacing,
should she stay down or should she surface?

Should the saleswoman
return first the call from the name she knows, or
return first the call from the name she does not know?

Why do we solo, service providing businesswomen,
working as attorneys and accountants,
so often include
"and associates"
in our business name,
when there are no associates and
thus we know that at the moment
when the customer ceases being fooled
we will lose the customer's trust?

What are the arguments
for and against utilitarianism, that is,
always doing the greatest good
for the greatest number?

Does the percentage of society which is interested in
Eternal Questions change?

Are there any new Eternal Questions?

Is the number of Eternal Questions finite?

(Both you, the reader, and I, Iwanna,
better hope so!).

When visiting a Grand Home,
is it preferable to pocket
a silver fork or a silver spoon?

Suburbs: Love 'em or hate 'em?

Bourgeois: Love 'em or hate 'em?

Should ethical systems begin
with intent or with conduct?

Should the doctor treat
with equal dispatch and skill
the DWI perp and
her equally injured DWI victim?

Why does Hollywood not aspire
for more than mere
shoot 'em ups,
titillation tails,
super-hero fantasies,
issue de jour propaganda attempts,
and sentimental journeys?[33]

---

[33] When Hollywood good girl Doris Day, whom one wag claimed to have known before she was a virgin, sang her signature song, *Sentimental Journey*, it was a different Hollywood time, and perhaps an Age of More Innocence:

> Gonna take a sentimental journey
> Gonna set my heart at ease
> Gonna make a sentimental journey
> To renew old memories

Can we imagine an actress singing that now?

When is pride sinful and when is pride virtuous?

How do we know
when to trust the data, and
when to trust the gut?

How do we personally fulfill
our natural and moral obligations
to the least of us?[34]

---

[34] Writing three generations ago, Robert Heinlein in *Stranger in a Strange Land*, a sci-fi story in which a Martian becomes an earthling, has Jubal, the leader of the Earthlings, say to one of his babes:

> Jill, of all the nonsense that twists the world, the concept of 'altruism' is the worst. People do what they want to do, every time. If it sometimes pains them to make a choice—if the choice turns out to look like a 'noble sacrifice', —you can be sure that it is in no wise nobler than the discomfort caused by greediness... the unpleasant necessity of having to decide between two things both of which you would like to do when you can't do both.

Ayn Rand was a mid-20th Century philosopher who promoted extreme individualism. She hated altruism and emotionalism, and she loved pure rationality. But in current times her magnum opus, *Atlas Shrugged*, has a greater appeal to impressionable teenagers than grownups. Also, when her real life lover ditched her for a younger model she became quite emotional indeed. The Stoics recommend all reason and no emotion, but why would anybody want to be Dr. Spock?

Stop crime — legalize drugs?

How do we balance
temptation and restraint?

How do we balance
faith, reason, feelings, fashion and superstition?

How robust is the inverse relationship
between an executive's ability to be a good executive and
the grandiosity of her office furniture and furnishings?

Do those who feel their way through life
find it a tragedy but
those who think their way through life
find it a comedy?

How may we pull out of our patterns of
Mary v. Martha and Virgin v. Slut, and
accept our own places
on our own curves?

What percentage of us,
in all honesty,
prefers a plate of quinoa over
a plate of buttery mashed potatoes?

How do we know the place and the issue
where we must stop going along to get along and
make a stand?

May atheists be both superstitious and consistent?

Should atheists
Beware the Ides of March?

Should we put reason as our source of the higher power?

What are the specific, if any,
excesses of the market?

On any given Sunday is
church more valuable than leisure, or is
leisure more valuable than church?

How do we balance
our duty to serve others with
our duty to serve ourselves? [35]

May a culture thrive
without religion?

Have any done so?

Do more sparkling dinner table settings
lead to
more sparkling dinner table conversations?

---

[35] The question whether one can simultaneously serve oneself and others brings up Immanuel Kant's bedeviling ideas about what he calls the "categorical imperative." Kant's categorical imperative suggests that all our actions should be taken with a view of whether doing the action in the particular circumstances at hand would be consistent with a benefit to society if all other persons in the same circumstances would take the same action, such as to create a "universal law." I, Iwanna, wish my philosophy Ph.D. candidate friends good luck in trying to figure that one out. Writing two generations ago Richard Weaver quotes Robt. E. Lee's definition of duty to others: "The sense of obligation to act as one would have others act, out of a love of order and accomplishment."

When we feel we are invisible, is it
because we are invisible, or is it
because we are allowing others
to define us as invisible, or is it
because we are defining ourselves as invisible?

Why does every bureaucracy have a
Department of Redundancy Department?

How do we know the standard
by which to judge our forebears?

Will our posterity judge us
any differently than we judge our forebears?

How may our faith not turn to despair?

On balance, does faith
make us better off or worse off?

Is it a proper function of government
to install a merry-go-round in a public park?

How about a beer hall, even if the locals love beer?

Is the Universe not only queerer
than we suppose,
but queerer
even than we can suppose?[36]

---

[36] John G. Neihardt asked this question in the May 1, 1928 issue of the *St. Louis Post-Dispatch*. Then, in an inexcusable concession to political correctness, Michael Guillen in the September 24, 2021 issue of the WSJ, asked the same question but swapped in the word "stranger" for the word "queerer." (What do we think of that?)

Why do women so often
let men talk them into
compromising their dignity?[37]

How and when does the smart woman reveal
her mystery?

If faith is so great,
why is so much evil done in its name?

How and when should
we let others serve us?

How would we view socialist states
if we put their potential to do harm
to the same standards of rigor
which the Food and Drug Administration uses
to judge new pharmaceuticals?

How long and how far must we go
to atone for our sins and mistakes, and
when is enough enough
so that we may let our errors go by the wayside
and we may proceed on our way?

Is it better to make the lunch appointment
for 11:45 or High Noon?

---

[37] At American colleges today there is a delightful phenomenon called "Naked Parties." It makes perfect sense that the boys want to have such parties, because virtually all males are obsessed with naked ladies. But I, Iwanna, see no sense in ladies, other than ladies in the profession, with whom I have no quarrel, agreeing to attend such affairs.

Is voting worth it?

Is going to church worth it?

How may a country develop its mores
such that its rulers value following its rules
more than winning on the issues?

Is it better to work in an organizational environment
where we have immediate wages and
more stability but surely less room to maneuver, or
is it better to strike out on our own in business
with surely no immediate cash and
surely less stability, but
with perhaps more upside and
surely more room to maneuver?

In war, as the battle deteriorates,
how does soldier or general know when
to give it up and fly?[38]

Why are societies based on rules better than societies
based on the discretion of even the wisest rulers?

In war may we kill civilians?

Just War? Total War? Any More?

---

[38] Writing forty generations ago, Anonymous in the *Song of Roland* writes of this dilemma:

> By God I charge you, hold fast and do not fly,
> Lest brave men sing ill songs in your despite.
> Better it were to perish in the fight.

Soon the grim reaper comes and "hales their souls away."

What do women want?[39]

---

[39] Many great writers have taken a crack at this one. Writing twenty-six generations ago, Geoffrey Chaucer in the *Wife of Bath's Tale* has the Wife argue for the woman to be in charge:

> Wommen desyren to have sovereyntee
> As wel over hir housbond as hir love,
> And for to been in maistrie him above.
> ...
> And eek I preye Iesu shorte hir lyves
> That wol nat be governed by hir wyves;

In Katherine's closing monologue in *The Taming of the Shrew* the Bard puts it a little differently:

> I am ashamed that women are so simple
> To offer war where they should kneel for peace,
> Or seek for rule, supremacy, and sway,
> Whey they are bound to serve, love and obey.

But maybe Kate is only being crafty in that speech and is really advising women only to pretend to "serve, love and obey" because that will be their most efficient path to "rule, supremacy and sway." That is the way modern directors handle it. But, I, Iwanna, confess that I don't believe that is what the Bard intended.

In this list I have avoided the TOP FIVE overworked Eternal Questions:

> If God is good why do bad things happen?
>
> Will there be peace?
>
> What is the meaning of life?

Does it always just come down to me?

Why when we grasp for it
does it elude us but
when we hold it loosely
it comes to us?[40]

Given that all women are mortal,
why are we so worried about death?

What to do when the neighbor's dog
keeps pooping in our yard?

Is every happy family alike and
is every unhappy family unhappy in its own way?[41]

Complain about being old after having had a fair chance?

How many angels can dance on the head of a pin?

If a tree falls in the forest and no one hears it does it make any noise?

But I make an exception for this overworked question, "What do women want?" because just as a moon brings a chuckle every time, this question brings a chuckle every time.

By the way, compliments of Saul Bellow, if someone asks you the eternal question "Do I exist?" you might respond "Who asked the question?"

[40] Confer, life partner hunting.

[41] Writing six generations ago, Leo Tolstoy begins *Anna Karenina* with that question framed as a statement.

Is it moral to supply an addict with funds and goods
which will end up being used
for gambling, sex, booze, drugs, and other depravity?

Why do the lazy remain idle?

Why do shunning and shaming
seem not appropriate responses
to the lazy and idle?

Or are shunning and shaming
appropriate to the lazy and idle after all?

What percentage of the lowest classes
are beyond help?

Why do so many in that class refuse help?

Should we always try to help?

Only sometimes?

How do we know when?

Who are we to intrude and claim we know?

How do members of our bottom strata
feel about us considering
ourselves "we," and
them "them"?

Are good shoes worth
more than
Seneca's books on Anger?[42]

---

[42] Writing seven generations ago, Lord Thomas Babington Macaulay, a British historian and sometime philosopher, asks this question and answers firmly yes.

May we accurately judge a movement
by how it treats its own members
who commit misconduct?

How do we navigate
between epicureanism and stoicism?

Does our humanity come from
100% nature *and* 100% nurture, or
are the percentages otherwise?

Is the core problem of racism
that it denies
Western Civilization's great advancement
of treasuring the individual
over the group?

Is so, should those who deplore racism
endorse Western Civilization?

Do missionaries from European religious traditions
who try to impose their traditions on peoples
who theretofore
had no knowledge of those traditions
violate those peoples' moral right
to their independent culture, or
do those missionaries
give those peoples an opportunity to
gain new knowledge and
to thereby make their own independent choices
from more options?

Should we aspire to be a subject matter enthusiast
on at least one subject?

If so, how does picking the subject relate to our parents?

Why do so many of us spend more
than our income?[43]

---

[43] Writing nine generations ago, Charles Dickens in *David Copperfield* has his profligate spending character, Mr. Micawber, address this subject this way:

> Annual income twenty pounds, annual expenditure nine-teen and six, result happiness.

> Annual income twenty pounds, annual expenditure twenty pounds ought and six, result misery.

Benjamin Franklin made money, and kept his income above his expenditures, by selling, among other things, "broadsheets", which were big posters to be plastered on walls as advertisements and for amusement. One such broadsheet was "The Art of Making Money Plenty":

> At this time when the general complaint is that money is so scarce it must be an act of kindness to inform the moneyless how they can reinforce their pockets. I will acquaint all with the true secret of money catching, the certain way to fill empty purses and how to keep them always full. Two simple rules well observed will do the business: 1st. Let honesty and labor be thy constant companions; 2nd. Spend one penny every day less than thy clear gains. Then shall thy pockets soon begin to thrive, thy creditors will never insult thee, nor want oppress, nor hunger bite, nor nakedness freeze thee. The whole hemisphere will shine brighter, and pleasure spring up in every corner of thy heart. Now thereby embrace these rules and be happy.

How do we steel ourselves
so that words will not hurt us?

How do we know
a white lie from a serious lie?

What amount of goods and chattels are
the right amount of goods and chattels
which one "should" own?

How do we know
when it is time to quit studying
our processes, procedures and approaches and
apply those processes, procedures and approaches
to actual problems?

If God exists,
does She have a special covenant
with all peoples,
with some peoples, or
with one people?

In school better to sit in the front, middle or back rows?

The difference between spending 2% more than one's income and spending 2% less than one's income is quite vast in a few years. The 4% reduction in expenditures would seem a pittance to pay for "result happiness" instead of "result misery," or as Franklin just put it, not having "nakedness freeze thee." Why the spendthrift gets jollies from thinking the saleslady at Saks has a high opinion of her because she is spending money is a mystery, for the saleslady uses her art to obtain commissions, and for no other reason. Confer also the Prostitute who pretends to really like the John.

If we receive an invitation
to a fancy party
just a few days before the party
should the insult of the lateness lead to a rejection, or
should we just go to the party anyway?

When we are in a tiff
how do we know whether to
discuss it with him face to face,
drop him as a friend,
steer clear,
apply the cut direct[44], or
pretend it is not happening?

How do we discern better vehicles from worse vehicles
when the styles are sportscars and pick-ups?

How do we discern better music from worse music
when the styles are classical and rock and roll?

For the religiously inclined
is there even value in trying to answer
the hard questions of the faith
such as whether God, (if God exists)
would have imposed predestination
if that would mean good people must go to the bad place
and vice versa?

Is it always true or only usually true that
when the performing arts become political
riveting stories become dreary moralizing?

---

[44] The "cut direct" is to see him with mutual friends and
pretend he is not there.

What percentage of partners in big law hate each other?

When our wise financial leaders
make pronouncements about M2, quantitative easing,
the velocity of money, temporary inflation, etc.
do they have any idea what they are talking about?

Do they think we are so foolish that we buy their bull and
believe they do know what they are talking about?[45]

Should elected officials control the money supply or
should independent groups control the money supply?

Will politicians ever stop inflating the currency?[46]

Will the modern military's prohibition
against the long-standing tradition of taking booty
stand up over time?

---

[45] Writing six generations ago, in *Roughing It* Mark
Twain puts it this way:

> Nothing in this world is palled in such impenetrable
> obscurity as a U.S. Treasury Comptroller's under-
> standing. The very fires of the hereafter could get up
> nothing more than a fitful glimmer in it.

[46] Writing six generations ago in *A Connecticut Yankee in
King Arthur's Court* Mark Twain has his benevolent
dictator say:

> So I had privately concluded to touch the treasury
> itself... I ordered a nickel to take the place of each
> gold coin, you see, and do its work for it. It might
> strain the nickel some, but I judged it could stand it.
> As a rule, I do not approve of watering stock, but I
> considered it square enough in this case.

When our organization or our family
suffers an oopsie from a faulty procedure
how do we decide
whether to enact a policy or
whether to just ignore the oopsie and proceed *ad hoc*?

To become a real intellectual
should our first topic of deep study be
the French Revolution?

If not, what?

Does recording events
in pictures, on audio and/or on video
so alter those events,
(unless the recording is clandestine),
that it should be avoided?

When *in media res*[47]
why is it so hard to accept
the reality of sunk costs?

How do we collectively stop ourselves
from murmuring among ourselves?

Is it even worth trying
to have one set of rules
for both the leaders and the people?[48]

---

[47] In the middle of things.

[48] A biographer of the mid-Asian Mongol leader, conqueror and terrorist Genghis Kahn says Genghis was the first to try it and that his descendants kept it going for a full 50 years after his death, which the biographer implies was then a new world record!

Are variations in character,
from mensch to sociopath,
spread evenly among the stations in life?

Is social shaming a fair way
to get those who know better
to comport their behavior
to the norms of social decency?

When we are being socially shamed how do we know
whether our accuser lacks good faith?

How may we control our minds so that
we judge ourselves against
our own aspirations and ideals
instead of judging ourselves
against the accomplishments, social shaming,
(and looks)
of others?[49]

Are we all journalists now, and
if so, how do we sort ourselves
between the good journalists and the bad journalists?

In a faith community
whose job is it to be sure that
all members of the congregation
know each other and care for each other?

---

[49] Writing eighty-five generations ago, Roman playwright Plautus, in his comedy *Pseudolus,* has his character Ballio, a pimp, say: "You can't do a man any harm by reviling him if he doesn't care a damn and doesn't try to deny what you say."

Is the only purpose of a trust fund
slightly slower dissipation
of the family fortune?

How long should family fortunes last?

What will be the effect
of the oncoming flood
of trust fund babies?

Will the oncoming flood of trust fund babies be
the biggest suckers of them all?

What are the trust fund babies going to do
when their spending, or inflation, wipes them out?

Do people in power *always* direct
the money mostly to their friends?

When standing in a creek bed
how many snakes are
within a 100-yard radius?

In foreign affairs
when does force make right?

In foreign affairs
when does justice make right?

How does a country's leader know whether or not
the other country's diplomat is a snake?[50]

---

[50] Writing forty generations ago Anonymous writes in the
Song of Roland, Dorothy Sayers translation:

But his true purpose – for that I cannot know
The French all say: "We'd best be very guarded."

When a woman plays with her house cat
is the woman more of a pastime to the cat
or is the cat more of a pastime to the woman?[51]

---

[51] Writing eighteen generations ago, French essayist and philosopher Michel de Montaigne asks this cat versus man question. Intellectuals have held Montaigne in reverence ever since, and he may well be one of history's great geniuses, but it is not certain whether more than a tiny percentage of these intellectuals have ever actually read any of Montaigne's essays, for they are slow going. (At least I, Iwanna, am certain the first few are slow going). We faux intellectuals like to make offhand references to "our pal Montaigne" as a way to show we are erudite, but most of us will be busted if anyone inquires with any depth into our knowledge of his fine points. Writing just now, Amor Towles in *A Gentleman in Moscow* makes perfect fun of Montaigne. The novel's hero over and over sits down to read his father's old copy of Montaigne's essays, and again and again the hero can't get past a page or two. Then in a clever plot maneuver the hero hollows out the pages of *The Essays*, and uses the hollowed out book to store valuables. Montaigne's book is thus more useful as a storage unit than as a book.

Writing four generations ago, James Joyce in *Ulysses* has his protagonist, Leopold Bloom, put it about the pussens this way:

> They call them stupid. They understand what we say better than we understand them. She understands all she wants to. Vindictive too. Wonder what I look like to her. Height of a tower? No, she can jump me.

Do animals have a sense of time?

Do animals ever ask one another,
"Where is our purpose now?"

Has any animal
ever contemplated her purpose at all?

Are animals bothered by
the closeness of heat in the summer and
the sting of cold in the winter?

If neither cows nor oxen
are contemplative,
what are cows considering
when they are standing by, and
what are oxen thinking
when they are standing round?[52]

---

[52] Once in royal David's city
Stood a lowly cattle shed

...

With the oxen standing round.

From Cecil Frances Alexander's *Hymns for Little
Children, 1848.*

You might have heard those lines during the entry
procession at Christmas-Time's Lessons and Carols.

Writing ten generations ago, Boswell in *Life of Johnson*
asks the question this way:

If a bull could speak, he might as well exclaim, "Here
am I with this cow and this grass; what being can enjoy
greater felicity?"

Would incessant petting
make a dog bored?

Do cows care about rainbows?

Do chimps ponder Eternal Questions?

As the horsefly
buzzes and orbits,
buzzes and orbits,
buzzes and orbits,
is she making facial expressions?

(How sweet is the stopping of the buzzing
when we smush her and she dies?)

How may we know any of these things about animals?[53]

Is murder ever banal?[54]

---

[53] Writing ninety-eight generations ago, Aristotle in the *Nicomachean Ethics* tells us that animals have no sense of purpose and cannot engage in contemplation. Montaigne takes the other tack asking: How do we know, by the force of our intelligence, the secret internal stirrings of animals? By what comparison between them and us do we infer the stupidity that we attribute to them?" I, Iwanna, with caution, go against Aristotle and with Montaigne on this one.

[54] Hannah Arendt coined the phrase "the banality of evil" for a *New Yorker* article she wrote while covering the Israelis' early 1960's trial and execution of Holocaust architect Adolph Eichmann for crimes against humanity, and Saul Bellow ripped her a new one for it in one of his novels, saying that everyone knows what murder is.

How would we go about setting up a school
where the self-disciplined, hard-workers would
not be treated as weenies by their
lazy bum classmates?

How may we steel ourselves
to try to be always wise and virtuous?[55]

Are free will and free bread
mutually exclusive?[56]

All in,
is there a tax rate which is just right?

All in,
is there a price of anything which is just right?

Over the Millennia
has there been a better financial wager than that
a gold piece will keep its value better than
a government backed bank note?

Why argue about verifiable facts?

But how blurry is the line between facts and opinions?

---

[55] Writing six generations ago, Mark Twain in *Huckleberry Finn* has Huck and Nigger Jim profess their allegiance to one another through what at the time were considered acts of immorality. Huck refuses to turn Jim back over to his owner, Ms. Watson, and saying: "All right, then, I'll go to hell," and Jim says: "I-I run off," but Twain draws each of those characters as the wisest and most virtuous of persons.

[56] Dostoevsky's Grand Inquisitor knows.

Does the greatest peace of mind
come through moments of total concentration?[57]

How may we control our minds
so that we will evaluate an idea
based only on the merits of the idea
and not on the merits
or even the biases
of the person promoting the idea?[58]

Is it even worth trying?

When asking a certain someone on a date
is it better to be general as in
"Will you go out with me this Saturday night?" or
is it better to be specific as in,
"Will you go see *Hamlet* with me this Saturday night?"

---

[57] Writing five generations ago, W. B. Yeats draws our attention to the concentration of Michelangelo:

There on that scaffolding reclines
Michael Angelo.
With no more sound than the mice make
His hand moves to and fro.

Like a long-legged fly upon the stream
His mind moves upon silence.

[58] Publius, in Federalist 40, tells us to ignore the proponent of an idea:

The prudent inquiry, in all cases, ought surely to be, not so much *from whom* the advice comes, as whether the advice be *good*. (Emphasis in original).

How would the study of herstory differ
if it were the losers who crafted the myths?

What percentage of us are doing
our own thinking, and
what percentage of us
are doing our thinking
as dictated by those we admire?

Should we hate more
the assassins of politicians or
should we hate more
the assassins of artists?

Why do some young adults
choose to engage in behavior
which will effectively
throw away their lives?

When does poverty result
from societal issues and
when does poverty result
from individual choices?

For those who think
it would be best to end
the American welfare system,
what arguments or events,
if any,
might be persuasive enough
to bring that about?[59]

Does commerce lead to virtue?

---

[59] Saving money is not the right answer.

Should we support the underdog
even in a circumstance
in which the overdog
has obtained her money, power and fame fairly, and
the underdog has chosen to be lazy? [60]

Why does the best approach
to running a family
seem so to differ
from the best approach
to running a government?

Is that the same sort of problem as why
the rules of physics at the scale of atoms
seem to differ so much from
the rules of physics at the scale of galaxies?

Why claim to be a helpless victim
when we can claim to be a rising survivor?

---

[60] Writing just now, Amor Towles in *A Gentleman in Moscow* touches this conundrum as he describes the initial meeting of the protagonist and the character who will become the protagonist's dearest friend:

> Sure enough, while Mikhail was prone to throw himself into a scrape at the slightest difference of opinion, regardless of the number or size of his opponents, it just so happened that Count Alexander Rostov was prone to leap to the defense of an outnumbered man regardless of how ill-conceived his cause. Thus, on the fourth day of their first year, the two students found themselves helping each other up off the ground, as they wiped the dust from their knees and the blood from their lips.

Is women's purpose
propagation of the species?

Is women's purpose
perfection of her spiritual being?

What is women's purpose?

After a lady has spent energy and time
perfecting her look and matching it to the occasion,
why does it seem against the rules
for a gentleman attending the occasion
to examine the result and
mention to her that it is working? [61]

What happens when every day for thirty days
a man tells a reluctant lady that she is beautiful [62]

Does Karma exist?

---

[61] I, Iwanna, curtsy demurely to the lady who at a social occasion displays her treasures just shy to the left and just shy to right of the majority position, and who, when the treasures are gazed upon, lowers her eyes, hunches forward her shoulders, bashfully covers up with her shawl, and walks away, only to soon thereafter raise back up her chin, let the shawl slip back, and push it all back out, all to promptly enter a fresh bouquet of victims where she will lower her eyes, hunch forward her shoulders, once more cover up with the shawl, and once more feign mortification... (Such is the power of pulchritude).

[62] Writing three generations ago, Malcolm X asks this question in both a realistic and a rhetorical manner. I, Iwanna, ask it only in a rhetorical manner.

Why do some of us not see
that when the roof is leaking
we must stop all other activities and fix the roof?

Do any modern dudes have more swag
than the TOP FIVE of
Franklin, Hemmingway, Bogart, JFK and Obama?

Who are the lady equivalents?

Have any wise guys given us
more to think about than the TOP FIVE of
Socrates, Shakespeare, da Vinci, Newton and Franklin?

Who are the lady equivalents?

For what clues should we watch
so we will know
when the volume of evil's roar
is increasing so quickly that
we must stop all other things and
pledge our lives, our fortunes, and our sacred honor
to fighting that evil?[63]

---

[63] Writing three generations ago, Supreme Court Justice
William O. Douglas, a tireless mid-20th century advocate
of free speech, hated by the right (thereby once more
proving that the right is often idiotic) puts it this way:

As nightfall does not come all at once, neither does
oppression. In both instances, there is a twilight
when everything remains seemingly unchanged.
And it is in such twilight that we all must be most
aware of change in the air—however slight—lest we
become unwitting victims of the darkness.

Is the jury the best way to both determine guilt and
innocence and
to find an appropriate balance
between punishment and mercy, and
is the jury also the best way
to balance the risk of the guilty being unpunished
the innocent being punished?

When the moment for action has arrived
why do we so often pause?

Do the ideas and thoughts of the aged
have greater intrinsic worth?

How much weight should we give tradition?

How should we balance
attention to the mundane with attention to
art, beauty, culture, Spiritualism
(or spiritualism), and
refined good taste?

Will attention to
art, beauty, culture, Spiritualism
(or spiritualism), and
refined good taste
improve the human heart?

Where is the straight path?

Messiah? Bread?

How do we know the line between acceptable jokes and tasteless jokes?[64]

May words express a complete idea?[65]

---

[64] At a gathering of whites in the Old South someone would tell a racist joke and everyone would laugh. Therein was enforced the then extant "code."

[65] Writing ninety-nine generations ago, Plato fusses with the meaning of words in his 7th Epistle in which he shows his disdain for one Dion of Syracuse, who had been both a tyrant and written a book on metaphysics. Plato condemned Dion for his audacity at writing about metaphysics (philosophy), for two reasons: first, because Plato believed that as a tyrant Dion could not be a serious thinker, and second, because Plato believed that words can never accurately describe anything anyway. Both arguments go too far, but let us examine only the second. If Plato really believed everything Dion wrote was waste because words cannot express truth, then Plato would have concluded that writing books was a waste of time and he would have stopped writing and spent his time enjoying whorehouses. Five generations ago 20th century philosophers Karl Popper and Ludwig Wittgenstein squabble interminably over whether words can express truth. I think Popper gets the better of it because he supports the idea that words seem to get the job done most of the time, while Wittgenstein responds that no one can understand anything. But the latter view is surely wrong because the study of philosophy does help us understand things and thereby makes us better women.

Is there a hippopotamus in the room?[66]

What is beauty and what is truth, or
are they the same?[67]

---

[66] During an early 20th Century debate among the smarties at Cambridge University Bertrand Russell asked Ludwig Wittgenstein if there was a hippopotamus in the room. Ludwig would not state a clear "No." Was the hippo behind him? Did he look? Ludwig was a con man.

[67] The Bard, substituting "honesty" for "truth" put it this way:

> Ophelia. Could beauty, my lord, have better converse than with honesty?

> Hamlet. Ay, truly: for the power of beauty will sooner transform honesty from what it is to a bawd than the force of honesty can translate beauty into his likeness. This was sometime a paradox, but now the time gives it proof. I did love you once.

Writing nine generations ago, Romantic era poet John Keats, cogitating on a one hundred generation old Grecian Urn, articulates an equivalence between truth and beauty:

> Beauty is Truth, Truth Beauty
> that is all ye know on earth,
> and all ye need to know.

I leave it to others wiser than I to answer whether the first clause's reciprocal is true, that is, whether:

> Ugly is Lying, Lying Ugly.

Is it good
to get good and drunk
at a wedding?

Is history made by a few heroes or
the floodtide of humanity?

What are the common threads
of the world's great religions?[68]

How may we banish our envy?

Grace, Faith or Works?

Does it matter?

If and when we pray does it matter
whether we do it alone or with others?

Everyone lies a little
so why such indignation over this and that little lie?

Should we judge a person
only by her deeds
or should we judge her
both by her deeds and her thoughts?

How can we be sure of her thoughts?

---

[68] Writing two generations ago, Huston Smith in *The World's Religions* asserts that the major wisdom traditions have the same don'ts and do's, with the don'ts well-expressed in the Decalogue and the do's well-expressed in the Golden Rule with additions of humility, charity and veracity. He adds that the wisdom traditions also tell us that we are born in mystery, we live in mystery, and we die in mystery.

Why do men seem to get up in the morning
seeking what they can get for themselves from others?

Why do women seem to get up in the morning
seeking what they may give of themselves to others?

Are the assumptions
behind the prior two questions accurate?

If the assumption behind
the question about women in the morning is accurate,
is the purpose of the feminist movement
to alter that aspect of the feminine condition?

What are the prospects for that purpose?

Is
DON'T SAY EVERYTHING YOU THINK
the best advice ever given?

Is
THINK FOR YOUR SELF
the best advice ever given?

If
SOME OTHER ADVICE
is the best advice ever given, what would that advice be?

Is it moral to give our time, attention and money
to artists, athletes and entertainers
who are morally bankrupt?

How may a nation advance its interests
without causing jealousies and uneasiness?[69]

---

[69] The phrase "jealousies and uneasiness" sounds odd to
our ear, but it is a quote from Federalist 4.

Should the fine points of traffic control
be handled by traffic experts or
by local elected officials?

Should the fine points of children's education
be handled by education experts or
by local parents?

Why do preachers give sermons
which sail past the twelve minute mark
when the hard science on the shape of the curve
from randomized, one variable, peer reviewed
double blind, replicated studies
shows unequivocally that after the twelve minute mark
the marginal number of souls saved
diminishes dramatically?

Does the hassle of becoming learned
pass the cost-benefit test?

How much knowledge of the humanities
must we have in order to put
great works of art
(and these Eternal Questions)
into meaningful context?

Is the greatest difficulty of becoming learned
that there is just too much to learn?

If it is worth it to try to become learned,
how do we select among the possible methodical
approaches to accomplishing that objective?

How may a great family
avoid regression to the mean, or
is that objective hopeless?

Have recent advances in offensive weaponry
made the world safer for democracy?

When we see a marauder approaching us
with obvious intent to harm us
will we react smartly?

During adulthood is it
better to stay put in one city and
achieve depth, or is it
better to move about from town to town
and achieve breadth?

From whence comes the beauty
of the golden ratio?

What is the ratio
of money spent by big corporations
sending out unread privacy policy notices
to money spent by big corporations
compensating customers for damages
from breaches of their privacy?

When a real intellectual
is asked to list her one hundred favorite books
why does she always include
ten everyone has heard of and
ninety no one has ever heard of?

Is it because she has really read
thousands of books and has carefully narrowed
her list down to a precious few, or is it because
she has read a few but not countless books and
she just wants to appear to be a smarty pants?

Is there a great novel whose first word is "I"?

What is the single greatest skill
offered by the greatest lawyers?

Cops? Military Personnel? Secretaries? Baristas?
Truckers? Doctors? Nurses? Clergy? Uberistas?

If the Buddha was satisfied with being able to
wait, fast and think[70]
why should we aspire to greater skills?

On a 1 to 10 scale,
as they dream of what should be our national objectives,
how closely do we all knowing and all wise ones think
the chattering classes and the common herd are aligned?

What if we asked representative members
of the chattering classes and the common herd?

What do representative members
of the chattering classes and the common herd
think of equality
as a national objective?

What do representative members of the middle class
think should be our national objectives?

How does the Artistic Director of the local Symphony
balance audience sensibility,
including the audience's desire for
Beethoven's Fifth Symphony at every concert,
with her desire to explore deeper into the canon?

When our lives are lonely and we want to change that,
how do we best make new friends?

---

[70] Writing four generations ago, Hermann Hesse in *Siddhartha* asserts those to be the Buddha's great skills.

Why white flight?

If we think our life has been a failure
should we still go to our class reunions?

In art how do we find stand firm in favor of
what we like ourselves and without regard to
what is popular with the general public?

In art may we determine what is good
by what the general public pays to read, see and hear
over the ages?

When either our loved ones or our business interests
are being held hostage by the bad gals,
do we pay the ransom?

In such circumstances are the authorities
our friends or our enemies?

After we have achieved our fame
how long will it endure?[71]

---

[71] Writing eight generations ago, Percy Bysshe Shelley quotes words which appear in an antique land on the pedestal of a colossal wreck of a statue of Ozymandias, King of Kings, whose shattered visage lies on the sand, half sunk:

Look on my Works, ye Mighty, and despair.

At all times the Whiffenpoofs sing:

We will serenade our Louie while life and voice
shall last,
Then we'll pass and be forgotten with the rest.

When we are getting into our 30's, still single, and
find our eagerness for marriage increasing,
what do we do about the problem
that most of the good ones are already taken?

How do we speed up Major League Baseball?

Should we go to the doctor
or just hope the condition will heal itself?

Keep open the public libraries?

Who decides what books
will be in the school library?

Why is it so damn hard
to just admit our mistakes, be sorry, and fix them?

Before heading off to the show
is it better or worse to quickly read *Hamlet*?

If we have led a life full of sound and fury
is our life still a tale signifying nothing?[72]

---

[72] Macbeth, the Scot, delivers the following just after the
death of his wife, Lady Macbeth:

Tomorrow, and tomorrow, and tomorrow,
Creeps in this petty pace from day to day,
To the last syllable of recorded time;
And all our yesterdays have lighted fools
The way to dusty death. Out, out, brief candle!
Life's but a walking shadow, a poor player,
That struts and frets his hour upon the stage,
And then is heard no more. It is a tale
Told by an idiot, full of sound and fury,
Signifying nothing.

Is porn free speech?

Were ancient nude sculptures, when carved and curved,
porn?

Can the average person manage her own life?

What are the chances that
our investment advisor's brilliant plan,
as she buys and sells and buys and sells,
always promising to beat the market,
will over our lifetime and our children's lifetimes,
particularly if we put her fees in the mix,
beat a plan of diversification, low fees, and buy and hold?

What are the chances that her brilliant plan,
particularly if we put in the mix her fees
and put in the mix the stepped up tax basis at our deaths,
will over our lifetime and our children's lifetimes
beat a plan of diversification, low fees, and buy and hold?

If the answers are obvious, why do we swing at her pitch?

Is the behavior of a country's leader driven
by her country's best interest or by her own egoism?

Must a country's leader be alert every single day
to the possibility
of invasion, aerial attack, and slaughter by her neighbors,
even by her neighbors she currently thinks of as friends?

Or is our modern world past all that?

When we are the boss of the committee
how do we control ourselves to keep our traps shut
until the underlings have offered up their best ideas?

Am I, Iwanna, a con woman?

How may we make our marriage
(or our life partnership)
the core of our lives, that is
how may we make our beloved
the source of our
deepest and most beautiful humanity,
so that we may
put our union first,
surely before children,
enjoy banter and laughter,
be secure in vulnerability,
never take advantage of vulnerability,
receive love,[73]
be more grateful for the good parts and
less disdainful of the bad parts,
keep our beloved informed of our whereabouts,
settle in for quotidian, leisurely, distractionless meals,
when grandma's china platter lies in shards
go quickly and silently for the broom,
exercise self-discipline and so
be not led into temptation, (and
not put ourselves in a position to be tempted),
provide for our beloved's

---

[73] Singing one generation ago in *Desperado* the Eagles give us ample warning:

It may be rainin'
But there's a rainbow above you
You better let somebody love you
You better let somebody love you
Before it's too late.

TOP FIVE basic matrimonial needs
on the distaff side
intimacy, security, respect, attention and gratitude, and
on the staff side
sex, food, tranquility[74], attention and gratitude,
during discussions say
"you're right" and "yes I will yes" and
then act on the yeses and I wills,
witness forgiveness,
avoid volatility,

---

[74] Writing eleven generations ago, Robert Burns warns that staying out too late may not lead to a warm greeting:

> When chapman bellies leave the street,
> And drouthy neebors neebors meet,
> As market-days are wearing late,
> And folk begin to tak the gate;
> While we sit bousin, at the nappy,
> And gettin fou and unco happy,
> We think na on the lang Scots miles,
> The mosses, waters, slaps, and stiles,
> That lie between us and our hame,
> Whare sits our sulky, sullen dame,
> Gathering her brows like gathering storm,
> Nursing her wrath to keep it warm.

In the Bard's *The Taming of the Shrew* Kate puts it succinctly:

> Fie, fie. Unknit that threatening unkind brow,
> And dart not scornful glances from those eyes
> To wound thy lord, thy king, thy governor.

not put our beloved in a position where
our beloved must pick
between us and the in-laws,[75]
endure and not criticize the in-laws,
for we know our beloved feels
about our family exactly
the way we feel about our beloved's family,
practice mutual loyalty,
and if the time to duel has
unfortunately but necessarily come
fire only into the air, or
better yet lower the weapon and
when the duel is over promptly ease
back into relationship,
hold off on the moralizing and
the silent treatment,
pleasure our beloved
with a plethora of pet names,
never say "calm down",
or worse, "pipe down",
always keep up the teasing and laughter and
defuse the tension with teasing and laughter,
when appropriate be a deaf, dumb and blind kid,
don't throw rocks for no reason,

---

[75] Naturally if the in-laws make the reciprocal mistake—making our beloved pick between us and them—it is appropriate for us to use this to our advantage, first, as an information gathering exercise, and second, as a way to drive an intentional wedge between our beloved and our beloved's family.

conjoin funds,
don't say "you are washing the dishes wrong,"
ask about and listen to descriptions of the day,
focusing less on the mundane and
more on lofty thoughts and on life's piquancies, [76]
don't keep score,
recognize that even helpful suggestions
are delivered at a cost,
keep second guessing to a minimum,
instead of letting nothing pass let lots pass,
for in common courtesy lies
the path back into relationship,
only start painting the kitchen
after asking our beloved for an opinion on the color,
like what our beloved likes,
including at least smiling while mixing
with our beloved's friends,
even if it must be with an involuntary smile,
don't too often tell our beloved what do to,
jump at spontaneous opportunity,

---

[76] Writing three generations ago, Tennessee Williams in *Night of the Iguana* has the operator of a rundown Mexican hotel describe her relationship with her recently deceased husband:

> Don't misunderstand me about Fred. I miss him, but we'd not only stopped sleeping together, we'd stopped talking together except in grunts—no quarrels, no misuderstandings, but if we'd exchanged two grunts in the course of a day, it was a long conversation we'd had that day between us.

keep hateful thoughts mum,
know intuitively not to crawl into bed
with curlers and a mask,
fake the libido as called for by the circumstances,[77]
adjust the impulses both
when impulses are throbbing with youth, and
when in middle age they are becoming more scarce, and
then accept the softening situation
as aging comes and impulses ebb and
our formerly nubile bods are
lumpy, bumpy, divoted and cracked,
drill down not with history lessons,[78]
do not question motives,
even in the face of contrary evidence,

---

[77] The sex part goes away this way, I, Iwanna, think, perhaps leading to marital horror, I, Iwanna, think. The woman isn't being satisfied because the man is selfish and insufficiently motivated to learn and practice certain skills, and one day he at least eyeballs another woman, and then his beloved cuts off him off from sex, maybe for the duration, and then without the sex part the relationship flags, and pretty soon we are merely roommates.

[78] A "history lesson" is a review of our beloved's past transgressions—all the way from last week's failure to put the socks in the hamper to an ancient improperly raised eyebrow. I, Iwanna, recommend the "24-hour Rule," as an antidote. The beloved combatants agree that any quarrel shall be brought forth before the first to drop off to sleep on the ensuing night, or on that subject the combatants shall forever hold their peace.

do not interrupt but instead
be attentive when our beloved is speaking,
be ever mindful that even modest criticism
and particularly a whiff of contempt
from our beloved stings like a bee,
support and not thwart our beloved,
compromise daily,
don't recoil from touch but instead
touch me,[79]

---

[79] Writing four generations ago James Joyce in *Ulysses* meditates on his TOP FIVE topics of: (1) our search for the divine, as first exemplified by the questions in the following quote: "Now who is that lanky looking galoot over there in the macintosh? Now who is he I'd like to know? Now I'd give a trifle to know who he is. Always someone turns up you never dreamt of" —with the answer being, I think, Jesus, as He was unrecognized by his disciples at Emmaus, and further exemplified in the book by the pain and pleasure of the elder protagonist, Bloom, at the instant of transubstantiation as the Eucharist is celebrated in the Catholic church nearby as he gazes and grazes on hottie Gerty MacDowell while she lies below him on the beach, and further emphasized by primacy, for the first sentence of the book reads: "Stately, plump Buck Mulligan came from the stairhead, bearing a bowl of lather on which a mirror and a razor lay crossed" —get it? "crossed," (2) fathers and sons, (3) physicality, (4) the raw deal received by the Irish at the hands of the British, and above all (5) what he calls in the book "that word known to all men", that is, "love". The younger of the book's protagonists, Stephen Dedalus, has the following thought

and at least try to feel
it is not out of obligation,
but out of opportunity,
for if our beloved isn't getting it at home
our beloved might be inclined or tempted
to get it elsewhere,
root root root for our beloved and

---

on that word known to all men, which echoes what scholars believe to be Joyce's thinking on the day he met his wife, the sexy Nora Barnacle:

> Touch me. Soft eyes. Soft soft soft hand. I am lonely here. O, touch me soon, now. What is that word known to all men? I am quiet here alone. Sad too. Touch, touch me.

Martin Luther King left a handwritten note card:

> Love is the greatest force in the universe. It is the heart-beat of the moral cosmos. He who loves is a participant in the being of God.

Singing two and a half generations ago, Jim Morrison of The Doors, (with their name "The Doors" taken from a William Blake poem about opening the "Doors of Perception") gives us:

> Come on, come on, come on, come on
> Now touch me babe.

Many have heard the wedding words from I Corinthians:

> And now these three remain: faith, hope and love. But the greatest of these is love.

Thus, *that word known to all men*, is — love.

help help help our beloved,
give our beloved love and adoration,
not consider our beloved words and ideas wrong
just because they come from our beloved and
when we are formulating an idea and
our beloved begins to act on an alternative idea
before we have spoken,
swallow our idea and
pivot immediately
(even though such pivot is as hard as a triple lutz) and
adopt our beloved's idea with enthusiasm,
for it probably doesn't matter and
a failure to pivot ends up in a wasted admonishment,
not consider our beloved's
method of doing something to be wrong
just because it is our beloved who is doing it,
over and over turn toward our beloved
even when we may rightfully turn away,
keep it fresh and never be complacent,
for the highly motivated, ever-present challengers are
young, vibrant, cheery, fawning—and
eager to steal our beloved right out from over us,
be gentle during his good cry,
not giggle too much during her macho blusteriness,
not scrutinize every little thing,
endure what commonly appears to be
an unreasonable division of labor,
all so as to ever seek the joy and
so ever knock off
those cunning challengers thinking of country matters,
willingly accept our own and our beloved's

sins, fault lines, and temptations,
smooch on greeting and leaving,
come home, every time,
shoot the television,
don't burn the house down intentionally,
make our beloved's life more pleasant,
connect in ways only we two know,[80]
peel away the anger,
don't say everything we think, and, finally,
because early patterns change not much, and

---

[80] Writing two generations ago, Dana Gioia writes in his poem, *Marriage of Many Years*:

Most of what happens happens beyond words.
The lexicon of lip and fingertip
defies translation into common speech.
I recognize the musk of your dark hair.
It always thrills me, though I can't describe it.
My finger on your thigh does not touch skin—
it touches *your* skin warming to my touch.
You are a language I have learned by heart.

This intimate patois will vanish with us,
its only native speakers. Does it matter?
Our tribal chants, our dances round the fire
performed the sorcery we most required.
They bound us in a spell time could not break.
Let the young vaunt their ecstasy. We keep
our tribe of two in sovereign secrecy.
What must be lost was never lost on us.

because we can't always get what WeWanna,
YET BE CONTENT?[81] [82] [83] [84]

---

[81] Touchstone in *As You Like It* says "When I was at home I was in a better place, but travelers must be content." Married people should make their home a better place so at home they may be content.

[82] In *Othello* the villain Iago tells the tragic hero Othello to "yet be content" with his wife, Desdemona. But Iago tells this to Othello only after Iago has wrongfully put into Othello's mind suspicion that Desdemona is having an affair. As the play goes along Othello gets more and more agitated over this accusation, and at the end he kills Desdemona as a punishment for her infidelity—only to learn that she has not been unfaithful after all. Othello then smites himself. Whether in these circumstances he could have "yet been content" is an Eternal Question.

[83] Singing for all time, Mick Jagger serenades us with:

I Can't Always Get What Iwanna

[84] Whew. Perhaps you have noticed that this marriage question is pretty long. Instead of dragging through it perhaps we can just take our marriage vows seriously:

Anglican: (From the Book of Common Prayer)

Priest to Bride: Will you have this man to be your husband; to live together in the covenant of marriage? Will you love him, comfort him, honor and keep him, in sickness and in health; and, forsaking all others, be faithful to him as long as you both shall live?

IS THE SINGLE MOST DOMINANT FACTOR
IN HUMAN HAPPINESS
WHETHER WE LOVE OUR SPOUSE?

IS THERE ANY BETTER JUDGE OF CHARACTER
THAN HOW WE PERFORM IN MARRIAGE?

IS HOW WE PERFORM IN MARRIAGE
A BETTER MEASURE OF OUR CHARACTER
THAN HOW WE PERFORM IN
BRIDGE, BILLIARDS, GOLF, LACROSSE AND TENNIS?

WHY JUST THE PREPPY GAMES?

WHY NOT SPADES, BASKETBALL,
SOCCER, BOWLING AND SOFTBALL?

Bride to Groom: In the Name of God, I, N., take you, N., to be my husband, to have and to hold from this day forward, for better for worse, for richer for poorer, in sickness and in health, to love and to cherish, until we are parted by death. This is my solemn vow.

Muslim: (According to theknot.com—one form)

Bride: I, _____, offer you myself in marriage and in accordance with the instructions of the Holy Koran and the Holy Prophet, peace and blessing be upon him. I pledge, in honesty and with sincerity, to be for you an obedient and faithful wife.

Groom: I pledge, in honesty and sincerity, to be for you a faithful and helpful husband.

**HOW DO WE POSITION OURSELVES
TO RECEIVE CUPID'S ARROW?**

**HOW MAY WE ASSURE THAT
OUR LOVE IS NOT TRANSITORY?**

WHAT IS IT TO BE A REAL WOMAN?

WHAT IS IT TO BE A GRACIOUS LADY?

WHAT IS IT TO BE A REAL MAN?

WHAT IS IT TO BE A GRACIOUS GENTLEMAN?

IS LAUGHTER THE CENTER OF LOVE?

WHAT IS LOVE?[85]

---

[85] Singing three generations ago, Sam Cook tells us:

> Don't know much about history
> Don't know much biology
> Don't know much about a science book
> Don't know much about the French I took
> But I do know that I love you
> And I know that if you love me, too
> What a wonderful world this would be

Also singing three generations ago, Robert Palmer tells us:

> Doctor Doctor, gimme the news
> I got a bad case of lovin' you
> No pill's gonna cure my ill
> I got a bad case of lovin' you

Writing three generations ago, Robert Penn Warren in *All the King's Men* touches this "What is love?" question:

I heard the match rasp, and turned from the sea, which was dark now. The flame had caught the fat of the lightwood and was leaping up and spewing little stars like Christmas sparklers, and the light danced warmly on Anne Stanton's leaning face and then on her throat and cheek as, still crouching, she looked up at me when I approached the hearth. Her eyes were glittering like the eyes of a child when you give a nice surprise, and she laughed with a sudden throaty, tingling way. It is the way a woman laughs for happiness. They never laugh that way just when they are being polite or at a joke. A woman only laughs that way a few times in her life. A woman only laughs that way when something has touched her way down in the very quick of her being and the happiness just wells out as natural as breath and the first jonquils and mountain brooks. When a woman laughs that way it always does something to you. It does not matter what kind of a face she has got either. You hear that laugh and feel that you have grasped a clean and beautiful truth. You feel that way because that laugh is a revelation. It is a great impersonal sincerity. It is a spray of dewy blossom from the great central stalk of All Being, and the woman's name and address hasn't got a damn thing to do with it. Therefore, the laugh cannot be faked. If a woman could learn to fake it she would make Nell Gwyn and Pompadour look like a couple of Campfire Girls wearing bifocals and ground-gripper shoes with bands on their teeth. She could get all society by the ears. For all any man really wants is to hear a woman laugh like that.

First Buddy Holly but then the Stones, The Dead and countless others, sing of love in *Not Fade Away*:

> I'm gonna tell you how it's gonna be
> You're gonna give your love to me
> I want to love you night and day
> You know my loving not fade away
> Well you know my loving not fade away
>
> My love bigger than a Cadillac
> I'll try to show it when you're driving me back
> Your love for me got to be real
> A-for you to know just how I feel
> A love for real not fade away

Singing one generation ago in *Landslide*, Stevie Nicks and Fleetwood Mac ask the final question, maybe referencing God in the sky, and surely referencing nature in the sky:

> Oh, mirror in the sky
> What is love?

Singing at their end, the Beatles put it this way:

> And in the end
> The love you take is equal to the love you make

Finally, the Bard shows what love is in the following sonnet embedded in *Romeo and Juliet*. The sonnet comes when the star-crossed teenagers have fallen in love at first sight. By the end of the sonnet they are both giggling like the teenagers they are. (I, Iwanna, note that the sonnet comes soon before the balcony scene when Romeo sees Juliet lean her cheek upon her hand and wishes he were a glove upon that hand that he might touch that cheek):

Romeo:

    If I profane with my unworthiest hand

    This holy shrine, the gentle fine is this:

    My lips, two blushing pilgrims, ready stand

    To smooth that rough touch with a tender kiss.

Juliet:

    Good pilgrim, you do wrong your hand too much,

    Which mannerly devotion shows in this;

    For saints have hands that pilgrims' hands do touch,

    And palm to palm is holy palmers' kiss.

Romeo:

    Have not saints lips, and holy palmers too?

Juliet:

    Ay, pilgrim, lips that they must use in prayer.

Romeo:

    O, then, dear saint, let lips do what hands do;

    They pray, grant thou, lest faith turn to despair.

Juliet:

    Saints do not move, though grant for prayers' sake.

Romeo:

    Then move not, while my prayer's effect I take.

                Kisses her...

    Thus from my lips, by thine, my sin is purged.

Juliet:

    Then have my lips the sin that they have took.

Romeo:

    Sin from thy lips? O trespass sweetly urged!

    Give me my sin again.

Juliet:

              You kiss by the book.

About Atmosphere Press

Atmosphere Press is an independent, full-service publisher for excellent books in all genres and for all audiences. Learn more about what we do at atmospherepress.com.

We encourage you to check out some of Atmosphere's latest releases, which are available at Amazon.com and via order from your local bookstore: